Animals of the Bible

A Rooster Book / October 1996
"Rooster Books" and the portrayal
of a rooster are trademarks of Bantam
Doubleday Dell Publishing Group, Inc.

ISBN 0-553-09767-9   LC: 95-077858

Rooster Books are published by
Bantam Doubleday Dell Books for Young Readers,
a division of Bantam Doubleday Dell Publishing Group, Inc.,
1540 Broadway, New York, NY 10036

Manufactured in Singapore for Harriet Ziefert Inc.

Animals
of the Bible

Illustrated by Letizia Galli

ROOSTER BOOKS

Bantam Doubleday Dell
New York • Toronto • London • Sydney • Auckland

ADAM AND EVE AND THE SERPENT

Adam was the first man. Eve was the first woman. They lived in a garden called Eden that God made for them. Eden was full of beautiful fruit trees so that Adam and Eve had enough to eat.

God said to Adam and Eve, "You can eat from all the trees in the garden except one. If you eat the fruit of the Tree of Knowledge of Good and Evil, you will die."

There were all kinds of creatures in the garden. The serpent was the cleverest. The serpent asked Eve, "Is it true that God said you cannot eat from all the trees in the garden?"

"Yes," said Eve. "God said that Adam and I may eat from all of the trees but one. If we taste the fruit of the Tree of Knowledge, we will die."

The serpent told Eve, "I do not believe that you and Adam will die if you taste the fruit from the Tree of Knowledge. If you taste its fruit, you will be more like God because you will know what good and evil are."

The fruit on the Tree of Knowledge looked delicious to Eve. She tasted the fruit and took some to Adam. He tasted the fruit too.

God saw what Adam and Eve had done. God asked them, "Is it true that you ate the fruit of the Tree of Knowledge of Good and Evil?"

"Yes," said Eve, "but I did it because the serpent tricked me."

God punished Adam and Eve. "Because of what you did," God said, "there will be sadness in the world." God made Adam and Eve leave Eden.

God punished the serpent too. "Because of what you did," God said, "you will be the lowest of all my creatures." God made the serpent crawl on his belly for the rest of his life.

"Now the serpent was more subtle than any beast of the field which the Lord God had made." Genesis 3:1

NOAH AND THE DOVE

God said to Noah, "I am going to make a great flood. It will destroy all living things on the earth. If you want to live, build an ark and put your family inside. Bring two animals of each kind, a male and a female."

So Noah built the ark. When it started to rain, he and his family and two of every animal got inside.

It rained for forty days and forty nights. The ark was tossed up and down by the flood waters. All the living things left on earth were destroyed.

One day, the ark landed on a mountain top. Noah wondered if he could go outside. He opened a window and peeked outside. Noah could not see any dry land.

Noah had an idea. He would send out a dove from the ark. If the dove came back, Noah would know that there was nowhere for the dove to perch. If the dove did not come back, Noah could be sure that the dove had found somewhere to nest.

Noah opened a window in the ark and let the dove fly out. But water still covered the whole earth and the dove came back to the ark.

Noah waited seven more days and let the dove fly out again. This time the dove came back with an olive branch in its mouth. Then Noah knew that the waters had gone down. The olive branch was a sign that there would be life again on earth.

Noah waited another seven days and let the dove out one last time. The dove never came back. Thanks to the dove, Noah knew that there would be life on earth and that the flood was over.

God spoke to Noah and said, "Go out of the ark and bring your family and all the animals with you. Be fruitful and multiply."

NOAH AND THE DOVE

God said to Noah, "I am going to make a great flood. It will destroy all living things on the earth. If you want to live, build an ark and put your family inside. Bring two animals of each kind, a male and a female."

So Noah built the ark. When it started to rain, he and his family and two of every animal got inside.

It rained for forty days and forty nights. The ark was tossed up and down by the flood waters. All the living things left on earth were destroyed.

One day, the ark landed on a mountain top. Noah wondered if he could go outside. He opened a window and peeked outside. Noah could not see any dry land.

Noah had an idea. He would send out a dove from the ark. If the dove came back, Noah would know that there was nowhere for the dove to perch. If the dove did not come back, Noah could be sure that the dove had found somewhere to nest.

Noah opened a window in the ark and let the dove fly out. But water still covered the whole earth and the dove came back to the ark.

Noah waited seven more days and let the dove fly out again. This time the dove came back with an olive branch in its mouth. Then Noah knew that the waters had gone down. The olive branch was a sign that there would be life again on earth.

Noah waited another seven days and let the dove out one last time. The dove never came back. Thanks to the dove, Noah knew that there would be life on earth and that the flood was over.

God spoke to Noah and said, "Go out of the ark and bring your family and all the animals with you. Be fruitful and multiply."

"Now the Lord had prepared a great fish to swallow up Jonah. And Jonah was in the belly of the fish three days and three nights." Jonah 1:17

THE WOLF AND THE LAMB

Long ago, in the land of Israel, there was peace and there was war. There was good and there was evil. Some people were strong and some were weak. Some were kind and some were wicked.

One day God said to Isaiah, "I will create a new heaven and a new earth so wonderful that what existed before will not be remembered by anybody. People should rejoice forever about this world that I will create, for I will create a Jerusalem that will be a delight, and its people shall be a joy."

Isaiah was happy to hear this. He looked up at the bright blue sky and asked God to tell him more.

God talked about the animals in this new and peaceful world. He said, "The cow will feed with the bear; the lion will eat straw like an ox; and the wolf and the lamb will feed together."

Isaiah imagined the wolf and the lamb eating peacefully, side by side. And he was pleased.

JONAH AND THE FISH

God spoke to Jonah and said, "Arise! You must go to the city of Nineveh and tell the people there that they must stop being wicked."

But Jonah did not want to go to Nineveh, so he tried to run away from God. Jonah boarded a ship sailing for Tarshis.

God sent a great wind out onto the sea. The wind made a storm so terrible that the ship nearly sank.

One of the frightened sailors said, "Let's cast lots and see which one of us is the cause of this storm."

They cast lots and the lot fell on Jonah.

"What evil did you do to cause this storm?" the sailors asked Jonah.

"I am running away from God," Jonah explained.

"What can we do to end the storm?" they asked Jonah.

"You can throw me into the sea," said Jonah. "I know the storm is all my fault and I do not want any harm to come to you."

God made a giant fish to swallow Jonah up. The fish opened his big jaws and ate Jonah.

Jonah was in the belly of the fish for three long days and three long nights. He prayed to God.

God heard Jonah's prayers and forgave him for running away.

God spoke to the fish. "Let Jonah out," said God.

And the fish spit Jonah out of his belly and onto dry land. Then Jonah went off to Nineveh as God had told him to.

"Then the king commanded, and they brought Daniel, and cast him into the den of lions. Now the king spake and said unto Daniel, Thy God whom thou servest continually, he will deliver thee." Daniel 6:16

"And she hastened, and emptied her pitcher into the trough, and ran again unto the well to draw water, and drew for all his camels." Genesis 24:20

DANIEL AND THE LIONS

King Darius of Persia had three presidents and one hundred and twenty princes. Daniel was his favorite prince.

The other princes and presidents were jealous of Daniel. They made a plan to get Daniel in trouble with the king. They wrote a royal decree that said no person could pray to any god except King Darius. Anyone who broke this rule would be thrown into a den of lions.

Daniel was at home praying to God as he always did. The king's men cried, "Don't you know about the new decree? You cannot pray to your God—only to King Darius!"

The king was angry with Daniel and ordered his men to throw him into a den of lions. The king said to Daniel, "Now only your God can save you."

Then the king sealed the den with a heavy stone so Daniel could not escape.

The next day the king returned to the lions' den. "Daniel, are you there?" he cried.

Daniel answered, "I am here. My God sent an angel to shut the lions' mouths so that they would not harm me."

Daniel was taken out of the den of lions and the men who got Daniel in trouble were put into the den.

"Let the lions tear them into pieces," said the king.

Now King Darius believed in Daniel's God. He decreed that everyone in the kingdom should bow down to Daniel's God, because his God was the only true God.

REBECCA AND THE CAMELS

Abraham wanted a wife for his son, Isaac. He sent his servant on a journey to Abraham's hometown to find one. The servant took ten camels with him.

When he reached the town, the servant stopped at a well. His camels were thirsty from the long journey and so was he. The servant prayed, "God, let the young women of the town come down to the well. If one of them gives me a drink of water from her pitcher and gives some to my camels, I will know that she is the right woman for Isaac."

Just then, a pretty young woman named Rebecca came down to the well. She was carrying a pitcher on her shoulder.

"Do you think I could have some water to drink?" asked the servant.

"Yes," said Rebecca. "You look very thirsty and so do your camels."

Rebecca filled up her pitcher and gave the servant water. Then she returned to the well again and again until the camels had enough to drink. The servant knew that Rebecca would make the perfect wife for Isaac. God had answered his prayer.

The servant asked Rebecca's father if his daughter would marry Isaac.

Rebecca's father asked, "Will you go with this man to be Isaac's wife?"

Rebecca answered, "Yes, I know that I am the right woman for Isaac."

Rebecca then rode with the servant back to Abraham's house to become Isaac's beloved wife.

"And the dove came in to him in the evening; and, lo, in her mouth was an olive leaf plucked off." Genesis 8:11

"The wolf will live with the lamb, the leopard will lie down with the goat, the calf and the lion and the yearling together, and a little child will lead them."

Isaiah 11:6-8